Samuel French Acting Edition

This Flat Earth

by Lindsey Ferrentino

SAMUELFRENCH.COM   SAMUELFRENCH.CO.UK

FOR PRODUCTION ENQUIRIES

UNITED STATES AND CANADA
Info@SamuelFrench.com
1-866-598-8449

UNITED KINGDOM AND EUROPE
Plays@SamuelFrench.co.uk
020-7255-4302

Each title is subject to availability from Samuel French, depending
upon country of performance. Please be aware that *THIS FLAT EARTH*
may not be licensed by Samuel French in your territory. Professional
and amateur producers should contact the nearest Samuel French
office or licensing partner to verify availability.

MUSIC USE NOTE

Licensees are solely responsible for obtaining formal written permission from copyright owners to use copyrighted music in the performance of this play and are strongly cautioned to do so. If no such permission is obtained by the licensee, then the licensee must use only original music that the licensee owns and controls. Licensees are solely responsible and liable for all music clearances and shall indemnify the copyright owners of the play(s) and their licensing agent, Samuel French, against any costs, expenses, losses and liabilities arising from the use of music by licensees. Please contact the appropriate music licensing authority in your territory for the rights to any incidental music.

IMPORTANT BILLING AND CREDIT REQUIREMENTS

If you have obtained performance rights to this title, please refer to your licensing agreement for important billing and credit requirements.

THIS FLAT EARTH was first produced by Playwrights Horizons at their Mainstage Theater on April 9, 2018. The production was directed by Rebecca Taichman, with sets by Dane Laffrey, costumes by Paloma Young, lighting design by Christopher Akerlind, sound design by Mikhail Fiksel, and music direction by Christian Frederickson. The production stage manager was Cole P. Bonenberger. The cast was as follows:

JULIE	Ella Kennedy Davis
DAN	Lucas Papaelias
ZANDER	Ian Saint-Germain
LISA	Cassie Beck
CLORIS	Lynda Gravátt

CHARACTERS

JULIE – Thirteen, looks as much like a child as a middle-schooler can. This is not what she wants.

DAN – Late thirties, Julie's father.

ZANDER – Thirteen, Julie's friend, made of long bones and acne.

LISA – Early forties, Noelle's mother.

CLORIS – Eighties, an air of mystery and strength around her.

THE CELLIST

Cast members can be any race and should absolutely reflect some diversity in this world.

SETTING

A probably East Coast, seaside town in New England.
Affluent down below near the water.
Poorer, older, more industrial the higher you go up the hill.
The play takes place in an apartment building on the hill.
A working-middle-class apartment building.
Two separate apartments on top of each other,
connected by a fire escape on one side, a hallway/staircase on the other.
A piece of sidewalk below the fire escape...
or something to represent the above.

TIME

A November of the not-so-distant past.

AUTHOR'S NOTES

A slash (/) indicates overlapping dialogue.

An ellipsis (...) as its own line indicates an impluse that wants to be articulated but isn't.

When Columbus lived, people thought
the earth was flat.
They believed the Atlantic Ocean to be filled with monsters
large enough to devour their ships,
and with fearful waterfalls
over which their frail vessels would plunge to destruction.
Columbus had to fight these foolish beliefs in order to get men to sail
with him...
And see the earth as round.

– Emma Miller Bolenius
The Boys' and Girls' Reader: Fifth Reader, 1919

*(From another place, **THE CELLIST** sits at her instrument, stretches her hands, and tunes her cello – one bow stroke at a time.)*

(Eventually the tuning melds into music, Bach's "Cello Suite No. 1" prelude as lights rise to the apartment above, where **CLORIS** stretches stiff hands and sets a record to play.**)*

*(In the apartment below, in her room, **JULIE** jolts upright in her bed and listens, holding a few of her stuffed animals.)*

JULIE. ...Are you there?!

Are you there...????

*(In the apartment below, Julie's father, **DAN**, enters his living room.)*

Are you there??

DAN. Told you I'd be here on the couch.

On the other side of the wall –

JULIE. – aren't you coming in?

DAN. ...Julie.

JULIE. One more night.

DAN. ...

JULIE. Dad, *please?*

*(**DAN** enters Julie's room.)*

Do you hear that?

---

*Licensees should use an arrangement of Bach's "Cello Suite No. 1" in the public domain.

**A license to produce *This Flat Earth* does not include a performance license for any third-party or copyrighted music. Licensees should create an original composition or use music in the public domain. For further information, please see Music Use Note on page 3.

DAN. – from the apartment upstairs.

JULIE. But –

DAN. Just some music.

JULIE. I know, but Dad –

DAN. She used to play all the time.

JULIE. She did?

DAN. Back when you were a kid.

JULIE. I still am one.

DAN. Okay...

JULIE. ...

DAN. ...

JULIE. I can't fall asleep.

DAN. I know.

JULIE. – but what's –

DAN. – rain.

JULIE. – what's that –

DAN. – tree outside.

    Wind's pushing it against your window.

JULIE. ...

DAN. You know what it is now, so you can't be scared, right?

JULIE. Well, what's that –

DAN. Truck, over metal grating.

JULIE. And what's –

DAN. Footsteps on wet pavement.

JULIE. And –

DAN. Thunder

    – but far away.

JULIE. And –

DAN. Traffic.

JULIE. And –

DAN. – siren –

JULIE. And –

DAN. The gutter dripping –

JULIE. And –

DAN. A plane going by –

JULIE. And –

DAN. Wind –

JULIE. And –

DAN. Rain.

JULIE. And –

DAN. We're in here.

And it's *all* outside...

> *(Lights focus on* **THE CELLIST** *furiously playing and then nothing.)*
>
> *(Blackout.)*
>
> *(Lights up.)*
>
> *(In Julie's room,* **JULIE** *and her friend* **ZANDER** *sit on her bed, watching a movie from a laptop.*)*
>
> *(***ZANDER** *reaches an arm around* **JULIE**. *She sees it. He retreats, acts like he was just stretching, focuses on the movie.)*

JULIE. How much did your laptop cost? I really wanna get my own.

ZANDER. It was free.

JULIE. *Free?!*

ZANDER. Well, my parents bought it.

JULIE. Oh.

ZANDER. SCARY MOVIE!!! AHHHHHHH!!!!

> *(***ZANDER** *places her foot in his lap, massaging it. They aren't in a place where this is normal.)*

JULIE. What're you doing?

ZANDER. I'm not sure.

> *(Movie. Something terrible happens onscreen.)*

---

*A license to produce *This Flat Earth* does not include a performance license for any third-party or copyrighted movies or recordings. Licensees should create their own.

JULIE. – look at your face!

ZANDER. What?

JULIE. – you big baby!

ZANDER. Hey, I'm not the one with stuffed animals all over my room!

JULIE. These are, they're not even mine, barely!

ZANDER. Can we maybe do something else...this movie is making me wanna barf.

JULIE. Oh come on, it's so fake, you know blood doesn't really look like that.

ZANDER. Stop –

JULIE. It's way more brownish and blobby.

Plus, people don't get shot, fall down, and *die* instantly. They have to bleed out first.

> *(***ZANDER*** jumps up.)*

...?

Um. – you cold? Got *cold* all of a sudden, didn't it?

> *(He throws a blanket at her.)*

ZANDER. That's why they call it a THROW blanket!

JULIE. Good one.

Come watch the movie with me!!

ZANDER. Okay.

> *(***ZANDER*** tucks ***JULIE*** in up to her neck.)*
>
> *(***JULIE*** sticks a hand out of the blanket, palm up... ***ZANDER*** sees the hand.)*
>
> *(Movie.)*
>
> *(Reaches out.)*
>
> *(Retreats.)*
>
> *(Movie.)*
>
> *(Looks back at that damn hand.)*

Should – do you want me t– can I hold your hand?

JULIE. Hm?

ZANDER. Nothing!

I. Didn't. Know if you were – Neverm– movie's awesome, actual– lovin' it.

(McDonald's theme.) Bad-da-ba-pa–

JULIE. Did you just ask if you / could –

ZANDER. No! No! – you just didn't put your hand in the blanket like I thought you would, but NO, it was more of a – little joke I'm playing with myself? I don't even see you like that!

JULIE. Oh.

...Okay.

...

Funnyyyy...?!

ZANDER. Yeah, I don't even see the girl body parts on you, so – not to worry!!

JULIE. I mean...

– they're there...!

ZANDER. I know, but since we've been spending time together lately since school stopped, you're like becoming a – sister to me. Like a. Little. Cousin. A gal-*pal-with-a-vagina.*

JULIE. Um.

...We're – *friends.*

ZANDER. I know! I know! Best friends!

(Movie.)

I uh. Like that skirt-thing you're wearing today... Skirt in front, shorts in back, how does that *work*, exactly?

JULIE. Why don't we *Only* watch this movie.

ZANDER. ...

JULIE. I know we held hands when they walked us out of school, but don't feel you hafta – I dunno – 'cause of that day.

ZANDER. No, no, I'm – I'm not anything!

JULIE. Plus vampires're totally my thing!

ZANDER. Me too.

We have so much in common.

JULIE. What I'm wearing is called a *skort*...actually?
  – they're shorts, but with – this extra flap –?

ZANDER. This is a real thing?

JULIE. Skorts are vintage. From the nineties.

> (**DAN** *enters the living room carrying cardboard boxes. He dumps them in the living room.*)

DAN. Don't come up here!
  I'll come back down to get 'em –

LISA. *(Offstage.)* I got it! Almost up.

DAN. – shit.

> (**DAN** *quickly straightens his apartment.* **LISA** *enters, more boxes in hand.*)

  – throw them anywhere. Would've been easier if we'd found parking out front! Sorry, should have said it was a walk-up. And your shoes!

> (**JULIE** *and* **ZANDER** *listen from Julie's room.*)

ZANDER. Julie, your dad's back –

JULIE. – you're *allowed* to be here
  – *not like we're hooking up.*

ZANDER. – clearly.

LISA. Stairs are a real workout, huh?!

DAN. We're used to it by now! We've learned it's never worth going back up for anything. Forget an umbrella, you just get wet.

LISA. Whew! Catch my breath!
  Your apartment's *beautiful*! / Lovely!

DAN. Well, it's not *your* house –

LISA. Please.
  A great couch –

DAN. I've had it forever.

LISA. I didn't realize you lived up this way –

DAN. Oh, yeah, we've been here awhile. Right after Julie was born actually.

You should try those stairs with groceries, who needs a gym!

(Weird adult laughter.)

JULIE. – why is my dad talking like that, he sounds like a *tool*!

DAN. Lemme help you –

LISA. You're like Ted – he'll take care of anything, as long as there's not a game on –

DAN. Haha – hysterical.

We men DO love sports.

LISA. Ted and I'll have you and Julie for a barbecue to thank you for delivering our orders –

JULIE. – who is *that*?

...Who's with / my dad?

LISA. Burgers, whatever she / likes.

DAN. Maybe, sure –

ZANDER. Does your dad have a girlfriend?

JULIE. Have you seen my dad? No way!

LISA. I'm not taking no...

DAN. Sure, / okay –

JULIE. That's – that's not, is that *Noelle's* mom??

ZANDER. No –

Why would she be here –

JULIE. I remember that voice from her speech today. Listen –!

*(**JULIE** and **ZANDER** move closer to the door.)*

LISA. You always say okay, then none of us see / you two –

DAN. That's not true –

LISA. You should join Ted's golf game with the other dads –

DAN. Oh, they go in the mornings, I work.

LISA. – go in late –

DAN. I – can't.

LISA. Well, they'd love to have you. Everyone says how funny you are.

At least come for dinner. As a thank you.

DAN. Uh, sure, sure, sometime – we'd love to.

LISA. I promise not to let Ted bore you with a tour of our wine cellar again. I am sure that's the last thing *you're* interested in.

DAN. Why? I like wine –

LISA. I know, I didn't mean –

His stupid beehives though? Come on.

That whole get-up he wears, he's my husband and I think he's ridiculous –

DAN. ...I like honey.

LISA. We're – just trying to – make a real effort to be – *social* again, even though it feels too soon –

– *probably always will* –

ZANDER. I think you're right.

JULIE. Oh God, oh / god!!!!

Why's she here?!

LISA. – sorry –

DAN. Not at all –

Let's – go get the last of the boxes from your car so you can be done.

(The adults exit.)

*(**JULIE** and **ZANDER** enter the living room.)*

ZANDER. Why was she *here*?

JULIE. *(Indicating the skort.) This* – I don't know if this is why she was here – but *this* skort, this was Noelle's...?

ZANDER. What.

JULIE. This...was.

ZANDER. ...What're you talking / about?

JULIE. Last year, when my dad and I were at Goodwill, I saw Noelle and her mom drop off some – of her clothes? – so I made my dad buy them all... This was hers!

ZANDER. Oh geez.

JULIE. It's not like we shop at Goodwill all the time! Hardly ever!!

ZANDER. – not about *that* –

JULIE. This was *before*. Not like I'd go buy her clothes *NOW*.

ZANDER. ...It's still creepy you wore it today. Why would you wear that?!

JULIE. – um, it's the nicest brand I have –? Do you think her mom noticed I wore it to the school dedication earlier? And that's why she's here?! Probably not, right?

ZANDER. *Why would you wear that?!*

JULIE. If people from the White House visit your town and you play violin for them, you hafta wear a good brand! Stop staring at my legs! / I said it was BEFORE.

ZANDER. I'm not! Why would I stare at your *legs*?!

JULIE. Forget it. Let's go put the movie back on.

ZANDER. – when we put my dog down, I carried his leash in my bookbag for a few months.

JULIE. ...So.

ZANDER. – maybe it's the same for you? – felt nice to – have it there.

JULIE. ...But you loved your dog. I kinda thought Noelle was really stuck-up...

ZANDER. Then why would you wear it?!

JULIE. I DON'T KNOW!

ZANDER. ...

JULIE. ...

ZANDER. ...Noelle did have really nice clothes.
What'll her mom and dad *do* with them now?

JULIE. ...What'll they do with her *bed*?

ZANDER. – turn Noelle's room into an office maybe? Or –

JULIE. Their house has like ten offices already.
Maybe a room for like crafts? Or –

ZANDER. Who has a room for *crafts*?

JULIE. Uh, Noelle's mom makes her own *pickles*, remember? – like – *why*. Why would anybody do that.

ZANDER. Fun pool party though.

JULIE. But – will they leave Noelle's room the same like she's away at summer camp forever? Or throw her stuff in the trash and pretend she never lived there?

ZANDER. ...

JULIE. ...

ZANDER. Uh –

JULIE. ...

ZANDER. ...The vice president had *the* worst breath!

JULIE. Oh my God!!

ZANDER. *(Chokes and dies.)* HORRIBLE.

JULIE. – the worst / THE WORST!

ZANDER. If I were vice president, I'd make my secret service brush my teeth. And like, shave me.

JULIE. Please, like you shave.

ZANDER. I *do*!

JULIE. Your toes maybe.

You have as much hair on your face as I do –

ZANDER. – 'cause I SHAVE!

JULIE. If I were president.

Which one day, I will be.

ZANDER. Obviously.

JULIE. I'd ask for.

I don't know, how 'bout world fucking peace?

And homeless people!

ZANDER. What about them?

JULIE. Just –

Don't have them.

Give them homes!

ZANDER. Yeah!

JULIE. And pizza, is just free.

ZANDER. *(Bad Italian accent.)* I'ma make you a special-a pizza!

JULIE. EW – WHAT IS THAT VOICE.

ZANDER. Special-a pizza.

JULIE. I'm dying, you sound like a Russian spy!

ZANDER. I *Italiano*!

JULIE. Ew – okay, stop.

Did you see before the dedication how the VP kept close-talking all the dead kid families –

ZANDER. Don't, god, / Julie –

JULIE. What?

ZANDER. *"Dead kid families"*?

JULIE. I'm making a joke.

ZANDER. There are things we shouldn't joke about!

JULIE. I'm saying all the dead kid families were holding tissues so it *looked* like they were crying...but they were probably only doing it so they didn't gag on the vice president's nasty-ass-shrimp-breath.

ZANDER. – yeah, you're the vice president.

Like, dude, buy a mint.

(**DAN** *enters, more boxes in hand.*)

JULIE. Dad, what are you doing?

DAN. – just –

(**DAN** *quickly puts the boxes down.*)

– just –

(**DAN** *exits.*)

ZANDER. That was weird. That was definitely weird. Wasn't it?

JULIE. Well yeah, duh, my dad's really weird.

...Hey, did you ever hear of this place in Japan where your boobs grow bigger without surgery?

ZANDER. Um...

Can't say that I have.

JULIE. The website says, one massage, they grow huge? I know you don't really see the girl parts yet, but I'm saving my allowance up to get to Japan.

ZANDER. Dude, how much is your *allowance*?

JULIE. I mean, I'm not gonna like – fly first class.

ZANDER. I only get ten bucks a week.

JULIE. You get TEN bucks?!
For *what*.

ZANDER. Clearing my plate? I guess it's like – my salary for being young?

JULIE. I get three bucks. Three. That's slave wages.

ZANDER. I don't think slaves got wages? Isn't that what makes you a slave?

JULIE. Well, three bucks is definitely illegal. Sweatshop kids make more than me. It's a joke, like – Dad, don't even bother. I'll be *forty* by the time I can afford my boob massage, then I'll be such an old lady, I won't even need it.

ZANDER. Yeah.

   …

…Ew, can you imagine being FORTY?

JULIE. So gross. My boobs'll be down past my knees, I'll step on them when I walk.

ZANDER. When I'm forty, I'll own a couple of mansions and have a wife and three kids and two dogs and a hamster and be rich and famous for discovering something –

JULIE. Discovering what? Like an island?

ZANDER. No, probably more like an app.

JULIE. Ugh, I gotta get to Japan!

ZANDER. Do you have to go all the way to Japan for that? There's gotta be somebody *here* who could – help with your problem –

JULIE. "My problem"?! I know Noelle's boobs were bigger than mine, don't rub it in!

ZANDER. Noelle again?! / You're obsessed!

JULIE. Everybody said Noelle's were big, when really she wore fancy bras with water and wires – when she took her bra off at PE the boobs were still in it – I saw!

ZANDER. *Julie.*

JULIE. If you saw her in the locker / room –

ZANDER. Noelle is the LAST female I want to picture naked, are you *kidding* me right / now?!

JULIE. At Noelle's funeral you could see her boobs above her coffin, remember?!

ZANDER. ...Now I'm actually gonna throw up.

JULIE. I've been picturing it the whole month we've been off.

ZANDER. Well *Don't*.

JULIE. I can't stop!

Out of all the funerals, hers was the only one with the coffin cover – thing open, how could you not notice?!

ZANDER. I just say to myself, "Don't think about it, don't think about it..."

Like adults do.

JULIE. I.

I have this theory, wanna hear?

ZANDER. Not really.

JULIE. My theory is –

– everybody with big boobs got shot and purposefully the flat-chested people were left alone.

ZANDER. ...

JULIE. I'm being serious. 'Cause – like – *why else would I be fine* –??

ZANDER. ...That's.

All of them were on the other side of the school.

'Cause they're in older grades.

Except Noelle.

And me and you didn't even know her that good.

JULIE. ...

ZANDER. ...

JULIE. Then *Why*...

ZANDER. ...

JULIE. ...

ZANDER. Sometimes – bad things happen – to put us on the path to the best things...

JULIE. What, did you read that on one of your mom's stupid bumper stickers? That's worse than my theory!

ZANDER. The principal said it at the school dedication earlier today, not me! Were you even listening?

JULIE. Of course not.

ZANDER. Well you should have been.

She – sort of – explained why this happened.

JULIE. So her theory is nine kids died so I can realize it's *good* to be flat-chested instead of planning my / trip –

ZANDER. You can't even afford a trip to Japan!

> *(Beat.)*

JULIE. ...Would you miss me?

ZANDER. Well, duh – I would.

JULIE. Like how you'd miss your cousin? Or how you'll miss all those boobs now that they're *dead*??

> *(A loud thud from above. **JULIE** screams, drops to the floor. **ZANDER** grabs her.)*

ZANDER. That wasn't –

JULIE. I know! / I'm –

ZANDER. That was nothing.

> *(They both look up.)*

JULIE. ...What *was* that?

ZANDER. I don't know. I've never lived in an apartment.

JULIE. Maybe the old lady upstairs had a *heart attack* and croaked.

ZANDER. – please, could you *please* stop talking like you don't care about people dying.

JULIE. I *do* care. But I'm not – *SAD* – are you?

ZANDER. ...

JULIE. *IT'S* sad, horrible, the WORST thing literally ever, but – I wish everybody would shut-up about how *sad* they are so they'd tell us why.

ZANDER. ...I cried more when my dog died. *Does that make me a bad person?*

JULIE. You knew your dog better...plus he could do so many cool tricks.

(*Together, they stare up.*)

ZANDER. – you don't think she – really?

JULIE. Before school, when we give the old lady my dad's paper, she makes him tell her a joke. And my dad has to read them off his *phone*!

ZANDER. Off his phone?

JULIE. And once, I saw where her teeth should be...except she didn't have any –

ZANDER. Stop trying to scare me –

JULIE. *You're scared?*

ZANDER. – are *you*?

JULIE. Literally never...

– but from the hall, her apartment smells like Windex and chicken soup.

And if you look closely, she has hair on her upper lip and spots on her hands.

ZANDER. ...Julie, I think you're pretty much just describing an old person.

JULIE. And the worst part is – she's been playing CELLO music, and Noelle played cello too, do you get how creepy that is?!

...You are freaking out!

ZANDER. Am not!

JULIE. Maybe she needs help –

ZANDER. How's that our problem? We're basically kids!

JULIE. We are going up the fire escape to spy on her.

ZANDER. The fire escape?!

Are you sure?

Have you ever done this before?

JULIE. No.

ZANDER. Shouldn't we get a grown-up? ...*Where are the grown-ups lately??*

JULIE. Let's go!

What'd ya – want me to hold your hand...?

ZANDER. I –

Let's do this.

> (**ZANDER** *takes* **JULIE***'s hand. They climb out the window and onto the fire escape.*)

JULIE. Ew, gross your hands're sweaty –

ZANDER. Shhhh –

JULIE. Come on, come on, come on, come on!!

> (*They go up the fire escape.*)

I wanna spit in that dumpster down there –

ZANDER. *Quiet voice* –

JULIE. – look-her-window's-open-a-little / *creepy*!

ZANDER. – *quiet*, we are supposed to be *sneaking* –

JULIE. – *all dark in there* –

ZANDER. – what're we even doing?! We're being so crazy! What are we even doing with our *lives*?!?

> (**JULIE** *places his hand directly onto her chest.*)

ZANDER. Woooah.

JULIE. You think my theory's true?

ZANDER. What?

JULIE. Think about it – Noelle.

Alice.

ZANDER. Julie, stop – SHH –

JULIE. Tom.

ZANDER. Tom was a guy!

JULIE. But he was a little fat.

ZANDER. ...

JULIE. – he was! – he had like –

ZANDER. That is not okay to joke / about.

JULIE.	ZANDER.
I'm not joking.	...
Halley.	...
Jillian.	Stop.

ZANDER. Stop – *how do you know all the names?*

JULIE. – they've been announced like a hundred times.

ZANDER. ...

JULIE.	ZANDER.
Etta.	*Stop.*
Sadie.	*Stop.*
Katrina.	Stop.
Sam.	*STOP!*

ZANDER. Shut-up, shut / up!!!

CLORIS. Is somebody out there?!

ZANDER. !!!

JULIE. Go-go-go!!!

> (**JULIE** *and* **ZANDER** *run down the fire escape as the adults enter, more boxes in hand.*)

LISA. Ted's office bought us a year of Omaha steaks!

DAN. You know men love meat!

LISA. – instead of sending us flowers –

DAN. Oh –

JULIE. Zander!

> (**JULIE** *indicates for him to be quiet and listen through the walls.*)

LISA. Now every Monday we get a new delivery, so. November's as good a time as any for a barbecue.

DAN. I – didn't know steak came in subscriptions!

ZANDER. How are those two still talking about barbecues?!

JULIE. Why is she *here*?!

ZANDER. Take your shorts things off, quick! Maybe she came for those.

LISA. – haven't had to grocery shop since – god knows when –

JULIE. Turn / around!

DAN. Well *that* sounds nice.

(**ZANDER** *packs his bag.*)

JULIE. You're leaving / me?!

ZANDER. – not gonna see you naked!

JULIE. No, don't go –

LISA. – that's been a real blessing I guess.

DAN. Definitely –

ZANDER. – see you when we go back to school tomorrow –

JULIE. No / don't go, please –

ZANDER. I can't be around sad people.

LISA. Funny story actually –

(**ZANDER** *enters the living room.*)

DAN. ALEXANDER!!

ZANDER. …

DAN. Come, *come* talk to us!! Please.

ZANDER. …

DAN. You know Noelle's – Mrs. Harris.

LISA. You can still call me Noelle's mom.

ZANDER. …my bike –

JULIE. …

(**ZANDER** *grabs his bike from the living room floor.*)

DAN. Why's your bike in the hallway? Don't you have a lock for outside?

ZANDER. Last time I was in your neighborhood, somebody was trying to cut it off.

DAN. Oh! – he's, he's kidding!

LISA. Nice to see you!

ZANDER. …

  …

  …

LISA. Bye Alexander.

> (**ZANDER** *rushes out of the apartment.*)

I only wish the reporters on my lawn would clear away that fast. Beanpole, isn't he?

DAN. – keeps shooting up!

LISA. So Julie's home? I didn't realize.

– sorry, I thought you said she was at a friend's. I'd love to see her...? Say hi.

DAN. She's –

JULIE. *(From the bedroom.) I'm sick!!*

DAN. She's been under the weather.

LISA. That's okay, I get it if she doesn't wanna –

DAN. No, really, she's been, she's staying up all night, nerves maybe?

She's not been well.

> (**JULIE** *makes coughing and sneezing sounds.*)

Julie get out here. *Now.*

JULIE. One second!

> (**JULIE** *changes her clothes – slipping on pants, hiding the skort, and throwing it into her trash can.*)

DAN. What. What were you saying. A funny story? Steak –?

LISA. Oh! – *two shipments* of steak were delivered before Ted and I noticed. We had stopped going out altogether. Didn't leave our house for the rest of October – but that steak kept coming, until Ted said, *"What is that smell?"* When I finally figured it out, the bottom ripped out. Wet rotten raw meat went pouring all over our doorstep. – little bloody packages everywhere.

DAN. ...

– what a – *great* story!! – funny –

LISA. I thought it was a sign.

DAN. A sign of *what*?

LISA. …I don't know. But lately, I'm constantly looking for them.

DAN. …Yeah.

…Julie?!

Come say hello!

– right now.

> (**JULIE** *pokes her head out into the living room.*)

LISA. Hi there!!

JULIE. …

LISA. How are you, honey. Are you – are you doing okay.

JULIE. Fine, just – been in there – wearing my *pants*.

DAN. What?

LISA. You played beautifully today.

I hope you'll continue with orchestra.

You are a very, very talented young lady.

JULIE. Oh – just a violin. I'm not even first.

LISA. Meant a lot to see you guys up there. To everyone, to the town.

Meant a lot to me.

JULIE. …Okay.

LISA. I hope you and your dad'll come over soon –

JULIE. Where?

LISA. You're welcome any time, we were just talking about setting a date, hopefully sometime this month, before Thanksgiving –

JULIE. Where?

Wait – To your *house*?

Why would I go to your house again?

DAN. *Julie.*

LISA. For dinner –

JULIE. No, I don't want to, Dad, do I have to?? That's creepy.

DAN. *(To* **LISA.***)* I'm / so sorry –

LISA. No, don't, / don't even, I –

DAN. *(To* **JULIE.***)* Yes, of course you have to –

LISA. No, honey, you don't have to –

DAN. Julie, please apologize –

LISA. It's fine, don't apologize –

DAN. Julie, *apologize.*

LISA. No, / no –

JULIE. Dad, I don't feel so good –

(**JULIE** *rushes out of the room.*)

DAN. I'm gonna talk to her, that was not –
I'll talk to her, this is not – she doesn't normally. Jesus – I'm so sorry. Genuinely.

LISA. Is there a storage closet or?

(**LISA** *goes to move boxes.*)

DAN. – those boxes are Julie's, actually. – trying not to – mix them up with Noel– with yours.

LISA. Right. I didn't –
I want to finish up here and go home.

DAN. I already told you, I'll deliver them for you, you shouldn't have to deal with this.

LISA. You know what, this is ridiculous. I practically – cornered you in the school parking lot *sobbing*! This isn't fair – you don't have room for all these – and you shouldn't have to run around for us, delivering the orders.

DAN. No – it's fine – No trouble, whatsoever.

LISA. When you offered in the school parking lot, I thought you'd store 'em in a *garage* –

DAN. – we've got it.

LISA. I thought you'd have more *space.*

DAN. – they're tins of fundraising popcorn, Lisa. We can handle it.

LISA. ...

DAN. ...

LISA. I didn't mean – I – I – I love this view. You can see the whole town!

DAN. Can see down to the water, on a clear day.

LISA. So flat down there, you can see everything.

– church, grocery store, the green – that's what sold us when we chose to live here. After house hunting, Ted and I went for dinner in town, you know, tables outside, the little Christmas lights. We kept going, "I don't know, do we do it? Do we move?" And then there were these – kids, barefoot, actually – running around chasing fireflies. I kept joking our realtor paid them to be there. I'm still not convinced she didn't.

DAN. – looks good lately. Nice, all those benches people just donated, that memorial fountain they're building, all those volunteers planting flowers. Doesn't even look like November now, looks like spring.

LISA. Wish it wasn't cloudy, so I could see my house –

...Looks tiny, doesn't it?

Like a little fake town...

(*Beat.*)

Julie's – Julie's not one of the lottery students, is she? I never realized.

DAN. ...Oh! No. We're sort of right on the district border. But she – we didn't have to join the lottery.

LISA. – thank God. I hear it can be a real frenzy.

The bus comes this far up?

DAN. I work for the water company. So I just drop her on my way. I'm sure it does. Just sort of our special morning routine. It's not far.

LISA. ...

DAN. We *like* living up here.

LISA. Of course! And I bet you got a great deal!

Well. I can't thank you / enough –

DAN. It's cool –

LISA. – the thought of bringing these in our house – or – going door to door where Noelle and I were taking orders – Throwing them away seemed –!

(Breaking down.)

What am I – We were *just* taking orders together.

DAN. ...

LISA. – sorry –

DAN. No, god, no, please!! Please.

LISA. ...

DAN. Can I – can I get you coffee, or –?

LISA. *Coffee?*

No. *No.*

I'm going.

DAN. Was nice to see you, Lisa.

Your speech today was – powerful stuff.

LISA. We – don't have to do that dinner, okay? November gets crazy anyway, with Thanksgiving –

DAN. No, it's – it's a nice / offer –

LISA. Let's not, I don't want to make Julie uncomfortable, that's the last thing I / want.

DAN. I will talk to her.

LISA. You're off the hook.

DAN. Oh...?

LISA. Take care.

> **(LISA** *exits.)*

> **(DAN** *turns toward Julie's room, takes a breath, and starts moving boxes.)*

DAN. Julie, come, come out here now, please!

> **(JULIE** *steps into the living room.)*

...?

JULIE. I'm not going there, Dad. It's creepy.

DAN. Sometimes – you have to do things that make you uncomfortable.

That's basically all being an adult is. Just one awkward social interaction after another.

JULIE. ...

...But I'm *not* an adult.

DAN. Well, it's part of growing up then.

You have to say things when you don't know what to say. Talk to people you don't wanna talk to. Be in uncomfortable situations – *all* of the time. Make decisions you don't understand. Do you understand me?

JULIE. I'm sorry...?

DAN. I wasn't looking for an apology.

We're all just – trying to do nice things.

JULIE. What was she doing here.

Why was she *here*.

No one *ever* comes here.

DAN. She was just helping me carry up your orders, for orchestra. That fundraiser popcorn you sold, remember? You sold so much, it took up both our cars. This is all yours.

JULIE. I sold *this* much and didn't even win...?

DAN. Win what?

JULIE. Remember?

Top seller won this awesome bubble machine.

You could have bought some.

DAN. I did buy a tin. And it *was forty dollars*. For popcorn. Do you know how much popcorn is? We could plant a cornfield for that.

JULIE. You told me –

DAN. I could buy a tractor to farm that cornfield.

(**JULIE** *laughs*.)

JULIE. A tractor? Really, Dad?

DAN. That price, I could buy a whole farm.

Move us out there...

JULIE. ...

DAN. Do you know what joke you wrote when you were a little kid, about tractors – I almost did it on stage.

JULIE. I wrote a joke – about tractors?

DAN. Oh yeah, you had lots of farm material.

You said – *"What did the farmer say when he lost his tractor?"*

JULIE. What?

DAN. "Where's my tractor?!"

      *(**JULIE** laughs.)*

JULIE. Pretty good.

DAN. Right?

JULIE. ...Can I have some?

DAN. Not before dinner.

– thought it'd be fun to order Chinese –

Our back-to-school tradition –

JULIE. We just did in September – so we're not doing that – ever again.

DAN. Oh.

JULIE. Not now. And not next year either.

Never. Again.

DAN. ...

JULIE. ...

DAN. ...

– big day tomorrow!

      *(**THE CELLIST** sets her cello, **CLORIS** sets her record and opens the window.)*

Everything'll be the same, everybody's first day back again, same as you...

      *(**THE CELLIST** plays Bach's "Cello Suite No. 1" – the rest of the prelude.*)*

JULIE. Dad, *why is* –

DAN. Don't worry, just music.

      *(**JULIE** looks up.)*

---

*Licensees should use an arrangement of Bach's "Cello Suite No. 1" in the public domain.

DAN. Did you hear at the school dedication today, they found everyone's backpacks, put them on the back of the same chairs... Repainted the lockers the same shade of green. They reset the classrooms down to the placement of a pencil so *nothing* is different.

      (**DAN** *opens boxes.*)

JULIE. Will I still have to give my Columbus report?

DAN. ?

JULIE. The one due the day it happened...

DAN. ...I don't know...

JULIE. *You don't know?*

DAN. I have never – *done* this before either...

But they guarantee it's the safest school in America...

Same teachers. Same desks. Same chairs.

They kept everything exactly the same.

So it feels like – it never even happened...and it'll be okay.

      (**DAN** *offers popcorn to* **JULIE.** *They sit staring out the window, eating popcorn for dinner.*)

      (**THE CELLIST** *plays and plays.*)

      (**JULIE** *goes into her room, pulls the skort out of the trash can, looks at it. She climbs out onto the fire escape toward the music. She throws the skort over the side.*)

      (*In a separate light, a moment suspended in time: as* **LISA** *is walking away from the building, her dead daughter's clothes fall down on her.*)

      (**LISA** *is stopped by this. She looks around and up, confused but recognizing it.*)

      (*The music plays.*)

      (*Blackout.*)

      (*The next morning.*)

      (**DAN** *and* **JULIE** *at Cloris' front door.*)

(From his phone.) Oh yeah, here's a good one – This is funny, this is really, really funny –

(Telling a joke to **CLORIS.**) Two old friends run into each other walking their dogs, decide to grab beer, but the bar – there's a big sign out front that says NO PETS. One of the friends ignores it and says, "Eh – Just follow my lead!"

Guy makes like he's blind, goes right in with his golden retriever, says, "This is my seeing eye dog!"

Manager says, "Right this way!"

Second guy tries to go in with his chihuahua.

Manager says, "Hey, no pets!"

Guy says, "But this here's my seeing eye dog!"

Manager says, "You expect ME to believe a chihuahua's your seeing eye dog?"

Guy goes, "WHAT? They gave me a *fuckin' chihuahua*?!"

CLORIS. A chihuahua?! That's / good!

JULIE. Oh my God, Dad. So embarrassing.

CLORIS. *(To* **JULIE.**) You should hear the filthy ones he tells me when you're not here.

DAN. – your paper, *madame* –

CLORIS. *(Takes the paper.) Gimme that –*

DAN. – let us know if you need anything.

CLORIS. *(Looking at the paper.)* Do you know any kids in the picture?

JULIE. What / picture?

DAN. – no. Come on, let's head out –

CLORIS. Aren't you in the orchestra?

JULIE. – there's a picture of us?!

CLORIS. With the vice president.

JULIE. Lemme see! I wanna see!!

DAN. I – We – have to go –

CLORIS. Hey, watch yourself. Kid-free zone in here.

*(***CLORIS*** hands the paper to* **JULIE.***)*

JULIE. ...

Oh.

...

...

Look, from the dedication yesterday, Dad.
I'm that one...

CLORIS. On the front page!

DAN. Let's give her back the paper – / and –

JULIE. Why didn't you tell me?

DAN. – 'cause you're in the back, you can hardly see.

JULIE. Shouldn't we put it on the fridge?

DAN. Julie, no, I don't think so, that feels wrong. Hand it /
give –

JULIE. What does this headline / mean?

DAN. Nothing –

JULIE. – what does it mean *Another*.

DAN ...

Give Mrs. – it means nothing – Julie, let's go, we'll talk
downstairs –

JULIE. *Dad* – Why does it say *Another*.

> (**JULIE** *runs downstairs into her apartment.*)

CLORIS. I'm sorry, I didn't mean to cause anything –

DAN. It's okay.

Thank you, here you go, have a nice day!

> (**DAN** *hands the paper to* **CLORIS***, who closes
> the door. He follows* **JULIE** *downstairs and
> into the apartment.*)

...

JULIE. ...

DAN. ...

JULIE. ...

Why did it say *Another*?

DAN. ...

JULIE. Has this happened before?

DAN. ...

JULIE. ...Dad, has this happened before?

DAN. ...You must know it has.

JULIE. Why would I *know* that?!

DAN. Not here, but this isn't – no, this isn't the first time something like this, how did you think –

JULIE. I don't like – watch the news!

DAN. Julie – yes.

Of course this has –

JULIE. If this has happened before, why would everybody be acting so shocked?

DAN. ...

...

Oh, well –

JULIE. How many times.

DAN. Julie. I don't want to talk about this, / please –

JULIE. How many!

DAN. If you want me to walk you into school, we need – Get your / coat –

JULIE. Like once before?

DAN. ...

JULIE. ...

Like five?

...Five times?!

DAN. Yes, sure –

JULIE. ...

Ten? ...

More?

More than that?

DAN. I don't know!

JULIE. Dad, more than ten? No way.

DAN. I don't know the exact number. It's always changing.

JULIE. ...What?

DAN. ...

JULIE. So why don't the grown-ups just *fix* it?!

>   *(Long beat.)*

DAN. ...

>   ...

>   I am not sure.

JULIE. ...

DAN. How can I cheer you up?

JULIE. *I'm not sad!!* Why is the only thing anyone wants to talk about is whether or not I'm sad. I am NOT SAD. I just don't see why I should go back 'til it's fixed.

DAN. What?

JULIE. Think about it.

>   That plan makes no sense.

>   Why would I go back to school if the problem isn't fixed?

>   Until then, why should I?

DAN. ...

>   ...

>   Because you *have* to.

JULIE. You didn't go to school.

DAN. Julie, I went to middle school. I didn't go to college, thanks for bringing *that* up, but it is not the same –

JULIE. I thought you *chose* not to go to college because you were *trying* to be a comedian.

DAN. Excuse me, I *was* a comedian.

JULIE. Do all comedians end up working at the water department?

DAN. ...

>   ...

>   Are you being mean on purpose?

JULIE. No. I'm really asking –

DAN. Why are we talking about. No, not – stop changing – I wasn't famous, but yes that's what I did when I met your mom, you know this already.

JULIE. 'Cause she was pretty so you noticed her in the front row? You made fun of her date's teeth and did your escalator routine...

DAN. I'm not.

JULIE. Could you – Please. I didn't mean to be mean to you. *Please...?*

DAN. Are you serious.

JULIE. ...

DAN. *Now?*

JULIE. I'm like super, super *sad*, Dad.

DAN. That is not / funny. We are running late now.

You know I can't be late or I'll be out for that promotion.

JULIE. Please? – please, please – *Pleaaaaaase!*

> (**DAN**, *behind the couch, mimes going down an escalator.*)

And the elevator.

> (**DAN** *mimes going down an elevator.*)

DAN. And then I'd. This is George W. Bush going down a broken escalator.

> (**DAN** *just stands there. Beat.*)

JULIE. ...

...

...I don't get that one.

DAN. Used to *kill* in the comedy clubs.

JULIE. – 'cause you used to be funnier?

DAN. ...

JULIE. I bet your jokes weren't like the ones you tell the old lady, you wrote them yourself and didn't read them off your phone –

DAN. When you were born, and suddenly it was just you and me, I couldn't think of them anymore. 'Cause there were much, much more – *important* things to think about...

Like getting you to school...

JULIE. I'll totally go back if you can promise what happened won't happen again.

Anywhere.

DAN. ...

JULIE. ...

DAN. ...

JULIE. *Can you –?*

DAN. ...

JULIE. Can you, Dad?

DAN. ...

    ...

    ...

        (He shakes his head.)

You can stay home.

JULIE. Really?

DAN. Today.

Only today.

JULIE. Thank you, thank you, thank you, / thank you!!

DAN. No, Julie, we're gonna have to – still – figure this out. How to get you – comfortable enough to – to go back...

JULIE. Dad, you're gonna be late.

DAN. We'll talk about this later.

Lock the door behind me. Put the chain on. And don't take it off.

I'm calling the house to check on you on all my breaks. Do not leave the front door.

    *(**JULIE** and **DAN** pinky swear. **DAN** exits. **JULIE** locks the locks...)*

    (She climbs out onto the fire escape...and up. Knocks on Cloris' window.)

CLORIS. What are you doing out there? Gave me a heart attack!

JULIE. My dad said not to leave our front door –

CLORIS. I'm pretty sure that he didn't mean go out on the fire escape!

JULIE. I just wanna – Can I see your paper again?

CLORIS. No, go home.

JULIE. Please.

CLORIS. ...Stay there.

Kids stay outside.

Adults in here. Kids out there.

Children do not come in, do you understand?

No kids past this point!

JULIE. I'm not a kid.

CLORIS. You are.

And all of this is not childproof.

Kid-free zone, you got it?

JULIE. Believe me, I'm not like – dying to come over.

CLORIS. So go home.

JULIE. I just wanna see your paper, please.

CLORIS. ...

Don't tell your dad. He has a number I don't want him calling. I have no desire to live with my idiot nephew who works at CVS and claims he's a *botanist*. I think we all know what he's really growing.

JULIE. I have *no* idea what you're talking about.

CLORIS. Don't tell him and we won't have a problem.

(**CLORIS** *gets the paper.*)

JULIE. What's your *name* –

CLORIS. I've known you since you were this big, what do you mean, what's my name?

JULIE. Sorry, I usually just call you the lady upstairs.

CLORIS. – Cloris.

JULIE. – *so cool*. My dad uses that to bleach our toilet.

CLORIS. – no, that's – no he doesn't –

JULIE. Why'd your parents name you that?

CLORIS. I have no idea.

JULIE. You should ask 'em.

CLORIS. They're dead.

JULIE. – really?

Are you sad?

Or did it put you on the path to the best things?

CLORIS. When you're old, everyone you know is dead. Some go to Florida, but that's pretty much the same.

(*Beat.*)

JULIE. Mostly everybody I know's dead too.

...My mom.

CLORIS. ...?

JULIE. And some kids at school, but I didn't really know them so, I'm fine.

CLORIS. ...Did your orchestra really play "Somewhere Over the Rainbow" for the vice president?

JULIE. They're releasing it on iTunes.

Album's called *Songs of Survivors.*

CLORIS. *Dear God.*

(**JULIE** *looks at the paper.*)

JULIE. ...Do. Do I actually look this sad, in real life?

CLORIS. You – do not look sad to me at all.

(*Beat.*)

JULIE. ...Thanks.

CLORIS. Can I get back to my / paper?

JULIE. Did you play that music last night?

And the night before?

CLORIS. You some kind of detective?

JULIE. I just really, really need to know if that was you.

CLORIS. Well, I've got tendonitis in my bowing hand and hemorrhoids now, so depends how you're defining "play."

Yes, I just started listening to my records again.

JULIE. But *why?* Why now, why suddenly. I need to know.

CLORIS. I was your age. Then I was married. Days go by. One day you're married thirty years. The next, he's been dead for ten.

JULIE. – I don't get it.

CLORIS. I don't either. But felt about time.

JULIE. ...

CLORIS. When you and your dad moved in, we thought one day I'd give you private lessons.

JULIE. Really?

CLORIS. But I sold my cello for a dishwasher, and you chose the violin, which everyone knows is an inferior instrument.

JULIE. *It is?*

I didn't know that.

CLORIS. A real musician carries twenty-five pounds on her back and plays that weight with a bow made of horse hair.

> (**CLORIS** *makes a cello with* **JULIE***'s arm: bent at the elbow, vertical to her chest.*)

A cello is as big and heavy as a human being.

You wrap your whole body around – so you're safe back there.

It leans on you.

I can still feel the weight against me.

Make this wide, open circle.

So you can bare down on the instrument with all you've got... Sink the bow into the string...

And bury the music into the floor.

> (**JULIE** *descends the fire escape, humming, air-playing her arm. She pushes two boxes into her room.*)
>
> (*She rips cardboard off the top, draws strings, tapes it to her chest. Stacks the boxes in front of her, sitting behind them for a makeshift cello.*)

(When **JULIE** *sits at the boxes,* **THE CELLIST** *plays.*)*

(A shift to later that night.)

*(***DAN** *opens the door to* **LISA**.*)*

*(***JULIE** *listens behind her cracked door.)*

DAN. LISA!

LISA. Hi!

DAN. Did you come back for your boxes? I haven't had a chance to deliver them yet, obviously –

LISA. No. And I don't intend on staying long.

DAN. ...? Well, come, come on in – water's great!

Do you want, can I get you something, a drink? A snack perhaps? We have plenty of popcorn!

LISA. Listen, I like you, Dan. I really, very genuinely do.

DAN. I – like you too – Lisa?

LISA. You've done such a good job with Julie. Julie's a great kid, this has nothing to do with – with anything.

DAN. – um, thanks – I'll keep her.

LISA. I'll just cut to it then. I came here to apologize for what I did.

DAN. What?

LISA. I'd like to walk you through it –

I volunteered in the front office? – at school, today. Parents were asked to spend time so there'd be friendly faces, I'm sure you saw the / e-mails –

DAN. Oh! I responded, I can't those hours – 'cause I'm at work –

LISA. – of course, you're as involved as you can be...

DAN. You're still going to school?

LISA. My son starts next fall. I will be as *involved* as is humanly possible.

---

*A license to produce *This Flat Earth* does not include a performance license for any third-party or copyrighted music. Licensees should create an original composition or use music in the public domain. For further information, please see Music Use Note on page 3.

DAN. Of course.

– can't even imagine.

LISA. Everyone keeps saying that to me.

I...

The thing is.

I *need* you to imagine it though.

That's – the only way you'll –

I'm not trying to be horrible or –

So I just need you to, please actually imagine it had been Julie.

JULIE. ...

DAN. Okay, that's – not.

LISA. If Julie had the bathroom pass, so was on the other side of the building where she wasn't even supposed to be.

– and when the school reopens, you don't know what to do. 'Cause you're used to driving there every day. Your morning routine. But now you don't have one. But you get dressed, *somehow*. You drive to school, even though your back seat is empty and you feel like an idiot, but you drive to your child's school, 'cause that is. *STILL*. My child's school. And always will be. And will soon be my son's!

But imagine now, you can't just go in, police walk you through metal detectors, search your bags, pull out a nail file you didn't know you had and you feel guilty for having a nail file. You wait, with the other volunteers for attendance sheets to be brought down to the office – by some child scared to walk down the hall.

You look at the attendance sheets to see who's absent.

Then pull up the file of every absent student.

Their address, phone number.

Every surviving kid who *chose* not to return to school...

DAN. ...Lisa – Julie was out sick. I told you yesterday she hasn't been / well.

LISA. That's why volunteers were asked to call parents, you know? Check in. Remind them we *have* metal detectors,

police checking guest passes, taking away nail files, we
know who should be there now, and who should *not*.

DAN. Lisa. Would you like to step into the hallway?

LISA. I called and I called all morning. I promise and
promise those parents no one will be around – *No One* –
who doesn't belong.

DAN. ...

LISA. ...

DAN. Is there something you're trying to say?

LISA. I could tell you were nervous yesterday.

DAN. I wasn't, no, you're always welcome –

LISA. You were uneasy –

DAN. *Uneasy?* Sure, yeah, maybe, obviously, I mean I've
been to your house –

LISA. So?

DAN. Well, I have eyes, Lisa. And so do you.

You host barbecues for the grade, we don't host play
dates! We don't even have a storage closet.

But me, being uneasy, doesn't *mean* anything.

LISA. We're getting away from why I came over.

DAN. Yes, *please*. Why are you here.

LISA. Julie wasn't there today –

DAN. I told you she was sick!

LISA. So I had to pull up Julie's school record.

Her phone number.

And address.

DAN. – okay.

LISA. – and unless – Julie lives in that *water department
office* and *NOT* here with you –

DAN. ...

What do you want from me.

LISA. *Address fraud is a felony.*

DAN. ...

...

...
Are you threatening us.

LISA. No, no, and I am sorry but I have to – I *have to* follow
the rules now.

DAN. We can talk about this –

I helped you out with your boxes, can we at least *talk*
about this?

LISA. There's nothing to talk about, it's done.

DAN. ...

LISA. I turned it to the principal, who turned it to the
school board earlier this afternoon. I just wanted to be
the one to give you a heads-up. And apologize.

DAN. ...

LISA. ...

DAN. ...

Okay.

I'd like you to please leave our house.

LISA. I keep promising those parents not even small things
will slip by –

DAN. I've been working to get things back to normal here,
this isn't easy for me to – but I'd like you to please leave
my house.

I don't think you heard me –

LISA. I *need* those same promises made to me. I need them.

DAN. Please get out of our house. *This is my house. Get out
of /* our house.

LISA. You would come back fighting.

And I will *fight.*

Until every last person who doesn't belong is *out.*

> (**LISA** *exits. Music plays as lights shift abruptly
> to the fire escape.**)

---

*A license to produce *This Flat Earth* does not include a performance
license for any third-party or copyrighted music. Licensees should create
an original composition or use music in the public domain. For further
information, please see Music Use Note on page 3.

CLORIS. Your body, from your head to your shoes, must stay relaxed, but strong.

JULIE. Tell me more.

CLORIS. …The range of a cello…is closest to the range of a human voice.

>   (**DAN** *moves boxes, punching them.*)

The upper notes are your yelling, your crying –

>   (*Plays the upper notes, back and forth.*)

…

Screeching, / shouting –

>   (*Lower notes, back and forth.*)

…

Down here, your complaining, despair –
It feels good to make a different kind of noise!

…

This is four, three – / two, one –

JULIE. Two, one –

>   (**JULIE** *air-plays to music. A knock at the door.*)

DAN. Are you kidding me?

>   (**ZANDER** *stands there with his bicycle.*)

ZANDER. Is Julie home?

DAN. This is *not* a / good time –

ZANDER. I need to see Julie –

DAN. She's in her room.

ZANDER. JULIE –!! JUUUULLLLIE!!!

CLORIS. Who is that?

ZANDER. Julie, I'm coming up –

CLORIS. Oh, hell no – He's not coming up here!

JULIE. Don't stop –

CLORIS. Go home.

>   (*The music plays on and* **JULIE** *descends the fire escape.*)

ZANDER. Julie – Juuuuuulllllie??

Julie?! Where were you?! I was looking for you all day! Are you sick?!

JULIE. I'm in the middle of something! You interrupted –

ZANDER. What could be more important than going back? You ditched me!

JULIE. I didn't ditch you.

ZANDER. Why? Is – is it 'cause I tried to hold your hand?

JULIE. No! I just couldn't go back – 'cause of what I found out.

Did you know this has happened before?

To other kids? At other schools?

ZANDER. ...

I mean – yeah, duh.

JULIE. Wait, what?

You did?

ZANDER. Duh, Julie.

Why do you think we're doing drills all the time?

JULIE. I don't know.

Those are *drills*!

ZANDER. No, Julie.

...You don't like – practice violin if you're never gonna play.

JULIE. What?

ZANDER. That's why we had to get really good at hiding.

JULIE. ...

ZANDER. We practice 'cause the adults knew it would eventually happen to us too.

JULIE. ...?

ZANDER. This one was just our turn.

JULIE. ...

...

What?

ZANDER. This happens like literally all the time.

JULIE. How'd you know?

ZANDER. I mean I know how to read.

I have my own cell phone and laptop.

JULIE. Shut-up, *mean*!

Don't rub it in!

ZANDER. No, no, don't get sad.

JULIE. I'm not sad!

ZANDER. It could be – good, maybe.

At least we got ours outta the way now.

JULIE. ...

ZANDER. ...

JULIE. ...

ZANDER. Here, I brought your bookbag. It was sitting on the back of your chair, exactly where you left it...

> (*Beat.* **JULIE** *picks it up.*)

JULIE. Oh.

Look –

My report I didn't get to turn in.

And – and – my lunch.

ZANDER. Ew, it's all rotten.

> (**JULIE** *holds the lunch and then throws it away.*)

How could you not show up? I really was looking for you all day. I had no one to talk to.

JULIE. Why're you shaking?

ZANDER. ...It's like hard to stand in front of somebody and say things you mean. You know?

JULIE. ...What?

ZANDER. ...

JULIE. – what is it?

ZANDER. – ever since that day I think about you, if I'm not with you? And if I am, I have to keep checking my hair and make sure I don't fall down – I dunno what to do with my hands, I find them here and am like, *What're you doing? Why'd you float up here?!*

Maybe bad things happened so we'd realize we're – *us*, ya know?

You and me.

This could be one of those – best things.

JULIE. What?

ZANDER. We'll – do this – then we'll BOTH feel better – I promise.

We – hear me out – should-just-jump-right-in-there, kiss! Get-it-outta-the-way-done.

JULIE. – oh.

...

...Okay.

ZANDER. ...Wait, seriously?

JULIE. Sure, I'll try anything at this point.

ZANDER. ...

I'll pretend you didn't say that.

...

...

Like – now?

JULIE. Well...not tomorrow!

...I'll wait. Here.

ZANDER. Comin'! I'm – on my way!

> *(Long beat. She closes her eyes. They wait...)*

JULIE. I'll.

Close my eyes, maybe.

> *(And wait.)*

> *(**ZANDER***'s paralyzed...)*

> *(He tries and tries and tries.)*

> *(Long beat.)*

ZANDER. *(A realization, disturbed.)* I – can't.

JULIE. *(Opens her eyes.)* ...?

ZANDER. I got scared *before*. But now –

(A confession.) It doesn't stop.

JULIE. ...

ZANDER. ...

JULIE. You weren't that day. You were like a – grown-up
then.

ZANDER. – I was?

JULIE. At the beginning of class. You helped me get down
my violin –

ZANDER. ...

JULIE. You knew to shut the closet door –

ZANDER. ...

JULIE. – put your arm – like –

> *(She gets under his arm.)*

– put my face – in your sweatshirt –

– but it was still loud, so –

> *(**ZANDER** covers her ears and holds her...
> An intimate moment that isn't necessarily
> romantic.)*

> *(**DAN** enters Julie's bedroom, and **JULIE** and
> **ZANDER** scramble away from each other.)*

DAN. Sorry.

JULIE. We weren't *doing* anything!

> *(**DAN** looks at both of them.)*

DAN. Believe me, I am *not* concerned.

...It's – getting late...

Julie and I need to –

Julie, we need to have a talk –

JULIE. I'll see you at school tomorrow. *I promise.*

DAN. Well, that's what we need to –

(To **ZANDER.***)* She may not be there for a little while – /
Just a little while longer –

ZANDER. What?

DAN. I'm sorry about that.

JULIE. No, no I'm ready to go back, Dad, I'll be there with
you, Zander – I *promise* you.

DAN. Um.

Well. No – Julie, you –

Can't right now – I gotta make some calls in the morning – and we'll see what the procedure is.

JULIE. *Procedure?*

ZANDER. – but she has to, she has homework, all her friends – plus, I have nobody to sit with at lunch –

DAN. ...I.

JULIE. Dad –?

DAN. I messed up, Julie. I think I maybe fucked up this time.

ZANDER. – what? –

DAN. Zander, please go.

JULIE. No, Dad, I want him here.

– stop looking like that –

DAN. This is hard – to – ...You can't go back to that school right now – that's it!

JULIE. You told me this morning I had to go back and I *want* to now.

DAN. – Not really about what you want, it's more complicated – you're not allowed, and if it turns out you are, great, but I don't know where you go in the meantime.

JULIE. Says *who* –

DAN. I ended up talking to Mrs. Harris, but –

JULIE. Noelle's mom?

ZANDER. She *kicked* you out?

DAN. No, no, she – she – sort of turned us in, Zander why are you still here?

ZANDER. – for Julie, sir.

JULIE. ...Dad, tell us.

DAN. ...

You...actually belong in that school up the hill – ? – but the building's older – there's no music program – when I toured it, there was a fight in the hall, so I tried – something else. Turns out maybe the other school would have been better? – but who'd have known. No one could have – You were never supposed to be down there in the first place.

JULIE. ...

DAN. Julie... Does, does this make sense?

JULIE. Is that why over summer everyone but us goes to Europe?

DAN. *Everyone* doesn't –

JULIE. *No one* drives to Wisconsin.

The only thing in Wisconsin is smelly cheese.

DAN. – that's the only thing in Europe, so.

ZANDER. – *our* family considers grandparent time *separate* from vacation time 'cause a vacation's *tropical* –

JULIE. – yeah, not the mall in Wisconsin which looks like the mall here.

DAN. *Why are we talking about this?*

JULIE. I'm saying I get it!

(*Beat.*)

DAN. ...

...You do?

JULIE. It's like when I bring my lunch, everybody gets goldfish, but you make me eat Dollar-Store cheddar whales.

DAN. What?

JULIE. And why I rent my violin from school when everybody else owns theirs so they can take it home to practice, when *I* have to practice in the music room after school and don't even get private lessons. Or have my own laptop or iPad or phone yet!

DAN. (*Furious.*) You know, when I was your age, Julie, I had a *job* –

JULIE. Now you want me to get a *job*?!

DAN. That's not – no –

JULIE. Why don't *you* just get a better one?!?

(*Beat.*)

DAN. ...

   ...

JULIE. I'm sorry –

DAN. ...

JULIE. Stop – looking – like that –

> (**JULIE** *mimes doing the escalator, but* **DAN** *doesn't laugh...*)

DAN. ...

JULIE. ...

Tell her I'll be really good at school. I'll stay on honor roll. I'll go to her house for dinner and never wear Noelle's clothes ever again.

DAN. Baby, that's not why this is happening –

JULIE. "Baby"?! I'm not a baby!

Dad, why can't you *do* something??

Dad, do something.

DAN. Like what?

JULIE. You're the adult, figure it out!

DAN. – we.

We need some time to – to make a plan. And think. You're staying home until I sort this out.

JULIE. You're asking me *not* to go to school.

DAN. I'm telling you – you can't!

> (**DAN** *exits Julie's bedroom.*)

JULIE. Where are you going?

> (**DAN** *exits the apartment, going to the hallway and eventually upstairs.*)

   ...

ZANDER. ...

JULIE. ...

ZANDER. Where'd your dad go?

JULIE. I don't know –

Why are there so many boxes?!?

(ZANDER and JULIE push the boxes out into the middle of the floor and start opening them furiously.)

JULIE. Noelle...

ZANDER. What?

JULIE. It says it's Noelle's...?

(ZANDER looks.)

Noelle.

(JULIE and ZANDER open one of the boxes. ZANDER pulls out a bubble machine with a large winner's ribbon attached.)

ZANDER. – You won the bubble machine? I didn't know you were the winner of the fundraising contest, I thought *Noelle* won.

JULIE. She did!!

(ZANDER drops the prize.)

ZANDER. ...Oh.

Then.

Why, why are they – *why is this / here?*

JULIE. Look –

(JULIE reads the forms from the boxes, getting gradually more upset.)

Noelle.

Noelle.

Noelle.

Noelle.

(ZANDER kisses JULIE.)

What?

ZANDER. How did that feel?

JULIE. WHAT.

ZANDER. Do you feel better.

JULIE. No.

Do you?

Tell me *you* do at least.

ZANDER. No.

Now what.

JULIE. I don't know.

ZANDER. Let's get rid of this stuff, we need to get rid of anything that reminds us of it – It needs to go – All of this NEEDS to GO – Should we throw it away?

JULIE. Do you think – do you think Noelle's mom wants it back?

ZANDER. What?

JULIE. My dad said she turned us in, so maybe –

Maybe we could trade with her.

ZANDER. Yeah, maybe she wants it!

JULIE. Like we'd give her these things and – oh, all of Noelle's clothes from Goodwill and –

ZANDER. And maybe she'll let you go back!

Yes, let's go tell your dad!

JULIE. No – no more waiting. No more listening to adults. Just you and me.

Her number's on all the order forms.

ZANDER. Should I call her and pretend to be your dad?

JULIE. You idiot, this isn't *The Little Rascals*.

We'll text her.

ZANDER. We make such a good team.

> (*He goes to kiss her but settles on a weird high-five-hug-slap-on-the-back thing.*)
>
> (**JULIE** *types into her phone.*)

JULIE. "This is Dan. I have your daughter's things."

ZANDER. Julie, that sounds scary.

"This is Dan. I have something of your daughter's I want to give you... It's really important." And I'm adding a smiley face.

> (**JULIE** *nods.*)

JULIE. Sent.

Wouldn't it be funny if I'd sent the little ghost emoji?

ZANDER. ...

JULIE. Kidding!
  Obviously.

ZANDER. Gimme that.

JULIE. I think I even have a pair of Noelle's shoes I bought
  that day.

ZANDER. Good, good. Great.

JULIE. Quick – put this away before my dad sees.

> (**JULIE** and **ZANDER** *push the boxes back into
> place.*)

ZANDER. "When"! She said "When"!

JULIE. – "Tomorrow morning. Before school."

> (**ZANDER** *types and hits send.*)

Be here early so we can go back in together.
And I'll get Noelle's clothes.

ZANDER. Don't worry... Our plan is gonna work, Julie.

> (**ZANDER** *exits.* **JULIE** *goes into her room,
> gathering Noelle's things and holding them.*)
>
> (**DAN** *on the staircase:*)

DAN. It's – me – sorry –
  Needed some space.

CLORIS. ...
  Got any jokes?

DAN. ...

CLORIS. ...

DAN. Why did the man leave his apartment?

CLORIS. Why?

DAN. To get away from your cello concert –

> (**CLORIS** *laughs.*)

CLORIS. – oh, you haven't said that one in awhile –

DAN. You haven't played music in awhile...

CLORIS. Never could hear myself over your cryin' baby –
  Everything alright downstairs?

DAN. ...

CLORIS. Damn these paper-thin walls.

DAN. ...

You know.

I took Julie fishing when she was a kid.

Had to google "how to fish" before we went.

I felt like CHECK ME OUT! Doing DAD things, like a dad!

...She took the hook...missed the worm...barb went in her finger!

There was blood, she was crying!

I go, "Don't worry." I'm like, I gotta make something up, to make her feel better.

So I say, "When a fisherman hooks his finger, that's a sign of good luck."

CLORIS. ...

DAN. ...

I was proud.

Like, "I taught you a LESSON! A DAD lesson." I thought I cheered her up! Did a good job.

Then. But then she took the hook... Stuck the thing right back in her finger!

(**CLORIS** *laughs.*)

CLORIS. ...

DAN. ...

CLORIS. I never was a kid person.

'Cause kids are what they are. Which is dirty and messy and leaving crumbs everywhere and always, always looking to you to know what to say. So I said, I'm not having any kids. Met my husband late... Who turned out dirty and messy and leaving crumbs everywhere and always, *always* looking to me to know what to say! Best thing I could do was tell him – Sorry, honey, I don't know. I know I love you, more than anything, but that doesn't help me know.

DAN. ...

CLORIS. ...

DAN. ...Yeah.

   ...

   ...

   – can't remember why I ever picked this place.

CLORIS. ...

DAN. ...

CLORIS. The view's not bad.

DAN. ...The view –

   Does not suck...

> *(Beat.)*

CLORIS. The best part of living where we are – is we can look at all of it.

   When you're down there, you probably can't even see how nice it is...

DAN. ...

   ...

CLORIS. Stay up here as long as you need.

> *(Cello music plays.*)*
>
> *(In her room, **JULIE** throws away her stuffed animals.)*
>
> *(**DAN** re-enters his apartment.)*
>
> *(**JULIE** is in her closed bedroom.)*

DAN. Julie??

   Julie, you okay?

> *(**DAN** knocks at Julie's door.)*

   Julie, you alright?

JULIE. What, Dad?

---

*A license to produce *This Flat Earth* does not include a performance license for any third-party or copyrighted music. Licensees should create an original composition or use music in the public domain. For further information, please see Music Use Note on page 3.

DAN. Oh, do – don't you need me to come in?

JULIE. …

DAN. *Can* I come in?

JULIE. Okay…

(**DAN** *enters Julie's room.*)

DAN. Are you –

How come you didn't call for me tonight?

JULIE. …It's just music, Dad.

DAN. Oh –

JULIE. – just a cello…

DAN. …

JULIE. …

JULIE. …

DAN. …

JULIE. …

DAN. …

JULIE. You know the bow is made of horse hair?

DAN. How'd you *know* that?

JULIE. The violin is an inferior instrument.

DAN. …Hm.

JULIE. …

DAN. – want me to stay 'til you fall asleep?

JULIE. …

DAN. …Can, I'm just gonna sit on your floor.

And –

And stay.

JULIE. …

DAN. I'll – I'll sit here.

And stay.

JULIE. …

DAN. …You're not scared?

JULIE. …

…

...

Of *what.*

> *(He sits on her floor.)*
>
> *(They listen to the cello music, which plays faster and faster and faster and faster.)*
>
> *(Quick light shift.)*
>
> *(Abruptly to the next morning.* **JULIE** *and* **ZANDER** *stand in the living room, with* **LISA** *in the doorway.)*
>
> *(***DAN*** enters a beat later.)*

DAN. What's going on?

ZANDER. Um, thank you, everyone, for meeting us this morning.

LISA. ...Uh, sure.

DAN. Zander, I live here, you don't.

Why are you answering my door? Go to school.

Lisa, you need something *else* –

You just love it up here now, or –

LISA. You texted me to come and pick something up –?

ZANDER. Um, well, no. You weren't texting with Julie's dad. You were texting with *us.*

LISA. Oh... Okay?

JULIE. Hi Mrs. Harris.

LISA. Thank you for – saying hi to me.

They said you found some things – of Noelle's –?

DAN. What did you two do?!

JULIE. We thought her mom'd want them back.

ZANDER. – but you gotta let Julie go back to school first. Then we'll give you all of Noelle's things.

LISA. Are you –

Are you *blackmailing* me?

ZANDER. No, no we're not blackmailing, we're *bribing*, it's different.

DAN. No! – you're not, *no*, they're not doing either of those things –

Julie, we will talk about this later, I haven't even called a lawyer yet / you should not have done this!

JULIE. Lawyer?!

DAN. Let me handle it!

JULIE. Why would we need a *lawyer* to change things, when we could change them ourselves?

DAN. I am the parent here, let me handle it!

JULIE. No! No one's DOING ANYTHING.

DAN. This just happened last night!

JULIE. No, no adults DO anything anymore. So I'm handling it myself –

DAN. Go to your room.

JULIE. Really? And what if I don't?

DAN. Go to your room. Now!

LISA. I should –

JULIE. I'm trying to be nice so you'll be nice back, that's not blackmailing, that's just how you taught me things go. Here, take this.

(**JULIE** *hands over the bubble machine.*)

LISA. What is this?

DAN. Where'd you find that?

JULIE. This cool prize Noelle won –
Noelle sold the most popcorn. She got first place and was really proud.

LISA. ...This is what I came here for?
This is what was so important?
This is it??

ZANDER. Everybody wanted it.

JULIE. – she was bragging about winning, Noelle was really proud, so – you should get to have it –

LISA. What?

JULIE. It's a really good one because it doesn't need to be plugged in. Look – here.

(**JULIE** *presses the button and bubbles blow and pop.*)

(Big beat.)

JULIE. – me and her barely talked –

ZANDER. Yeah, we didn't really know her.

JULIE. I was jealous she won, okay.
And how good she was at cello. You could tell she had private lessons. It's – not good to say, but I kinda started hoping something bad would happen to her.

DAN. Okay, that is enough! / You are done, stop talking!

JULIE. Not like this though. Like I hoped she'd trip or burp or get pimples on her back – but *not* – My theory is that what happened at school could be my fault.

DAN. Julie –

JULIE. – but I don't know, so if you hate me, I get it…so here!

> *(**JULIE** hands over the clothes.)*

– these are her clothes we bought at Goodwill, I don't want 'em anymore –

ZANDER. Julie, that's all we have left!!

LISA. What am I supposed to do with this?!?

JULIE. Let me go back to school –

LISA. It's not up to me –

JULIE. *Change it.* Or just *change* it, okay –

> *(**JULIE** grabs the clothes back and lays the pieces out one by one.)*

JULIE. Look at her shoes – and her shirt, and her sweater – Here, take it, take it – and –

LISA. I can't – it's already –

ZANDER. *Do something* –

LISA. *I can't* –

JULIE. – okay, okay – that day, that day she was complaining about her new shoes during orchestra. You might want to know she had blisters on her feet when she died. She probably didn't have them when she left for school so that's something you don't know about her – and – she had the bathroom pass not to pee, but because she would meet this boy on the other side of the school to make out with him...

LISA. What?

JULIE. Is that like, not allowed in your family?

LISA. No, I just, I didn't –

Really?

JULIE. – I thought you might wanna know.

LISA. I do – no, I do. Who was he?

ZANDER. – that tuba player? From marching band?

JULIE. Used to empty his spit thing on her shoes. She'd act like she was grossed out, but she laughed too.

LISA. ...

ZANDER. He came to her funeral –

JULIE. Yeah, he sat near us in the back –

ZANDER. – but he was mostly on his phone.

LISA. ...

...Oh.

...Well, thank you, I guess, / I –

JULIE. But, but I was also wondering about her toothbrush? – if you threw it away yet...and her hairbrush still has hair in it and how gross and weird and sad that is. And lip gloss touched her mouth before she died and her notebooks still have handwriting and there was homework she didn't get to turn in. Like none of us got to give our report that day even though we memorized it all weekend. This is my report I never got to give. And who picks clothes for the coffin and do you pick bras too and did she still have Band-Aids on her blisters in there. Do you wear shoes in a coffin? And do your hair and nails keep growing after you die? *And why do kids keep dying?!?* And are you mad you spent money on braces if her teeth never got straight and if when she was a baby you knew she'd only ever be thirteen would you have even sent her to school because *what's the point*, wouldn't you just rather hold her???? – did you know at her sixth birthday, her life was halfway done?

I don't know.

– she won this.

I didn't.

So I thought you should have it.

Take it, please. Out of here.

DAN. Sh.

> (**DAN** *holds* **JULIE.**)

JULIE. I'm fine!

DAN. Okay, alright –

LISA. …

   …

ZANDER. …

   …

JULIE. I had a skirt-thing of hers too, but I threw it off the fire escape into the dumpster down there –

LISA. You what?

JULIE. I'll go get it for you.

It's in the dumpster, but if you let me come back to school, I'll climb into the dumpster and get it for you.

LISA. You what?

That was you who threw that?

JULIE. Off the fire escape.

LISA. Of course you did.

I thought it was –

I don't know what I thought, but I –

I don't know what I thought –

Here's your report back.

I – I do want this.

And this –

And…

I want…

I want…

I want…

I want –

(LISA gathers what she can and exits.)

ZANDER. ...

DAN. ...

JULIE. ...

> *(A very long beat.)*

ZANDER. Wait.

> Wait, did our – did our plan – not work?

DAN. I'm sorry.

> I don't think so – no.

ZANDER. Should we come up with another plan, or –?

> Julie?
>
> I don't get it.
>
> I'll – see you at – school, or – or – or – We'll stay best friends, I bet. Right?

JULIE. Of course we will. See you soon.

> *(ZANDER exits.)*
>
> *(DAN picks up Julie's report.)*

DAN. Can I –

> *(JULIE nods.)*
>
> I mean, I'd still like to hear it –

JULIE. ...

DAN. If you had to memorize it.

> If you still remember –
>
> Come on –

> *(JULIE picks up the piece of paper.)*

JULIE. "...Mrs. Campbell asked us to read a book on Christopher Columbus and report on what we find interesting – so this, dear reader, is my report on Christopher Columbus and what I find most interesting."

DAN. Was there a word count you were trying to reach –

> *(JULIE laughs.)*

JULIE. No –?!

DAN. Sorry, don't stop –

JULIE. "Some say he's racist and pillaged and is basically the worst so we should *not* find Mr. Columbus interesting. But some say Columbus discovered the New World. Reading this book is confusing and occupying."

DAN. *Occupying?*

JULIE. The thesaurus said a synonym for interesting –

DAN. Just – keep going –

JULIE. "But *this* is what I *did* like."

> (**JULIE** *looks up. Lights shifting.*)
>
> (*She follows the music out and up.*)
>
> (**DAN** *picks up the paper and reads.*)

DAN. "A long time ago, people believed the earth was flat. Everybody asked where the edge was, but were too scared of falling off to try and get there. 'Cause – this flat earth...isn't flat at all.

Now we think it's funny they thought that, but really everybody was just always asking dumb stupid questions...

It is *occupying* to think – what're the questions *right now* that in the future people will laugh at us for not answering?

Maybe there's even a New World to find."

> (**LISA** *is collapsed, lost among the clothes.*)
>
> (**ZANDER** *rides his bike in place but gets nowhere.*)
>
> (*The sounds grow louder all around* **JULIE** *and the music draws her up and up the fire escape...*)
>
> (*The sounds grow louder and louder until –*)
>
> (*Lights out on everything but* **JULIE**.)
>
> (**JULIE** *bangs on Cloris' window.*)

JULIE. Are you there? *Are you there???*

(**CLORIS** *opens the window.*)

Can you tell me –

Am I supposed to play the cello?

Am I gonna be good?

CLORIS. If you want.

If you practice.

JULIE. Are you gonna teach me?

I'm supposed to learn –

CLORIS. What do you mean, *supposed to*?

JULIE. *I have a new theory.*

If everything at school didn't happen, I wouldn't have been awake to hear you play – Now you're supposed to teach me cello, and what happens next is we develop a life-long friendship. I make you nicer while you teach me the art of music.

CLORIS. Wow.

I don't know about all that.

It's just – the record is familiar.

So it relaxes me.

JULIE. ...That's it?

CLORIS. *That's it?*

You should have heard how I used to play...

JULIE. It must mean *something* though, right?

There has to be *some* reason.

CLORIS. If you like the sound, *fine* – but it's just – coming from a thing.

Made of wood.

JULIE. There's got to be a reason. That you play cello and so did Noelle.

CLORIS. Who?

JULIE. Or else –

How do you –

If anything can just *happen* –

How can anyone even get out of bed?

CLORIS. …

JULIE. I need to know what's gonna happen to me next. Tell me. *Tell me.*

CLORIS. You'll –

Go to high school after next year…?

JULIE. *Oh, come on.*

CLORIS. You'll start eating sushi then.

JULIE. Be serious –

CLORIS. You'll pretend to like it because you think you should…until one day you actually do. The same will happen with alcohol, museums and sex.

JULIE. …What will I look like? …

CLORIS. I'm sure you'll be taller…

It won't look good on you until suddenly you wear your own body well.

JULIE. *(Touching her chest.)* And what about *these.*

Tell me.

CLORIS. They may never grow.

JULIE. Are you serious?

CLORIS. But you'll learn not to care.

JULIE. And what about Zander –?

CLORIS. Is that some boy you like?

(**JULIE** *nods.*)

You'll eventually forget his name.

JULIE. *(Devastated.) What?*

CLORIS. You worry about running into him, but somehow you don't.

He grows long legs, big arms and a beard and by the time you do pass on the street, years from now, you don't even recognize each other.

JULIE. No.

There is no way that could…

No.

What else –

...
Tell me more. I can handle it.

CLORIS. I don't know –

JULIE. – what else...? Tell me. Tell me. Tell me. *Tell me.* **Tell me!**

> *(A sharp shift.)*
>
> *(Lights and time explode.)*
>
> *(The space between* **THE CELLIST** *and* **JULIE** *grows more infinite.)*

CLORIS. You and your dad plead to the school board.
There is no great fight.
Everyone's apologetic, but rules are rules.

> *(***DAN** *appears in the living room.)*
>
> *(***JULIE** *circles the perimeter of her apartment, watching him.)*

Your ride back from the hearing is very different from your ride there...
Your dad thinks of *home* as where he wants to be, but all you notice are bigger houses down the street.
Your dad tells a joke, but you stop finding him funny.
You go to the other school, and really it's not so bad.
Your dad never gets promoted.
You switch from violin to cello, but quit in tenth grade when it bores you.
And then –
You go away for college, come home less and less.
In your twenties, you fall in love with someone who doesn't love you back and you let this go on for longer than you care to admit.

JULIE. And –

> *(***JULIE** *is stopped outside her bedroom window. She can see the entire apartment and her dad lost amid furniture, cardboard, popcorn tins.)*

CLORIS. You cry. Scream. Actually pee yourself laughing on the third date with the man you marry – who is kind, likes to camp and reminds you, in secret, of the person you loved in your twenties.

JULIE. And –

CLORIS. Your love of spicy food grows until it gives you heartburn.

You stub six hundred toes.

Push out one son of your own.

JULIE. And –

CLORIS. Your dad fades away.

Hands first, jokes second, heart last.

You pick up the phone to call after he's gone, forgetting sometimes.

And when you smile in the mirror, you see your father's face, buried in yours.

And then, of course, the day comes when you pack up this place.

Turn your childhood *home* into – just some *room* – filled with boxes.

(*JULIE looks at all of the boxes in the room.*)

But...you'll have made your own family by then...

So you drive them here.

You go up.

And up.

Past the picnic table where you lose your virginity, the restaurant where you get your first job, burn your hand.

You don't mention what happened – at the old school.

And when you drive up to this building – it'll be knocked down, replaced with a Dairy Queen, but before you mourn its loss, your son wants ice cream.

JULIE. ...

CLORIS. You buy a house bigger than the one you grew up in and yet – there always will be bigger houses down the street.

Phones get smaller.

Traffic thicker.

Some countries invade other ones.

Some starve while others are fed.

And before you know it, the engravings on those memorial benches in town wear away with time until they are just some benches in a park.

No one remembers what the fountain was built for – or who planted those tulips, just that the fountain runs and the flowers come back year after year, until people say again – *"This. Is a pretty nice place to live..."*

JULIE. ...What are you talking about.

CLORIS. In your life, *this* is not the most important moment.

JULIE. *What?*

CLORIS. As you grow up, you learn that –

Terrible things – just, happen sometimes.

All we can do is get through it.

> (**JULIE** *considers this. And considers this.*)

JULIE. *No.*

That is.

That is not.

Not –

Good enough.

Not for this...

CLORIS. Pretty soon, you'll see...

You can come inside now, if you want.

> (**CLORIS** *opens the window for* **JULIE.** *A great wind blows through it.*)

You'll learn how to play.

JULIE. No.

> (**JULIE** *shakes her head and backs away from the window, toward the fire escape.*)
>
> (*She descends the stairs and stands there, elevated and alone.*)

(She shouts down into the apartment toward her dad.)

JULIE. Are you there?

*(**DAN** doesn't move.)*

*(She shouts below to **ZANDER** and **LISA**, each in their own light, together but separate.)*

Are you there?

(Still, no one moves.)

*(Lights circle in on **JULIE**, who looks out and out and out, straight into the audience.)*

Are.

You.

There.

(Quick blackout.)

End of Play